THE LOVE
I DON'T HAVE

By

Ramesh Mofleh Hussaini

1
Longing's Embers

In the silence, shadows sway Whispers of memories, gone astray A heart once full, now empty space Yearning for love, a distant place

If only I could turn back time Erase the pain, rewind the rhyme

But life moves on, and I'm left here With just a whisper, a lonely tear

In dreams, I see your gentle face A fleeting smile, a wistful pace

But dawn awakens, and you're gone Leaving me with this hollow song

If only love could heal the pain Bridge the gap, ease the strain

But love's a mystery, hard to define A bittersweet refrain, forever mine.

Ramesh Mofleh Hussaini

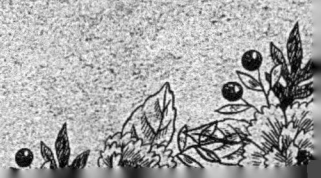

2
Lost in the Night

In streets of moonlit shadows deep I search for you, my heart
does leap The city's silence, a lonely hue

A canvas waiting, for memories anew

Your eyes, like stars, shone bright and true Guiding me through
life's uncertain tide But now, you're gone, and I'm left blue

A heart that's lost, with nothing to hide

The words I write, a futile refrain A poet's plea, in vain, in pain

Yet, I'll pen your name, in every line

A love letter, to your heart, forever mine

In this endless night, I'll find my way Through the darkness, to
a brighter day

Where love's warm light, will guide me home And in your arms,
my heart will find its own.

Ramesh Mofleh Hussaini

3
If I Were a Pen

If I were a pen, on the canvas of existence

I would draw lines of love and hope's insistence With my delicate and trembling tip

I would write stories of enduring legacy and unforgettable grip

In every line, a world of deep emotion and thought would lie And in every dot, a hidden secret of loving hearts would sigh With every stroke, a new and captivating tale would unfold

And with every punctuation, a fresh chapter full of mystery would be told

I would immortalize human dreams with my pen And turn their tears into smiles and joy again

My pen would be the eloquent tongue of loving hearts

And the voice of love, hope, freedom, and liberation's every part

With every word, a world of meaning and concept would unfold

And with every sentence, a life lesson and a loving message would be told If I were a pen, I would write with artistry and finesse

And with every line, a drop of the boundless ocean of love
would flow, I'd express

So my pen would be eternal, and my name would be recorded in
literary history's hall.

Ramesh Mofleh. Hussaini

4

"In moonlit streets, I search for you A heartbeat lost, without a
clue

Every step I take, echoes your name

But you're nowhere found, and I'm to blame

My heart beats fast, my soul feels pain Longing for your touch,
your love in vain

I'm a poet of your eyes, a slave to your gaze My words are
whispers, of a love that's dazed

In every verse, I pour my heart

A symphony of love, a work of art But without you, it's all in
vain

My pen writes only of the love we can't regain

Ramesh Mofleh Hussaini

5

"In whispers of wind, I hear your name A melody of memories,
a heart in pain The stars above, a canvas of dreams

A universe of longing, where love it seems

In shadows of night, I search for the light

A guiding star, to lead me through the fight The world outside,
a maze of unknown ways

But in my heart, a path that's lit by love's rays

In every verse, I pour my soul

A symphony of emotions, a heart that makes whole The words I
write, a bridge to the unknown

A journey through love, where heart and soul are shown

<u>Ramesh Mofleh Hussaini</u>

6

"In the vastness of space, we collide

Like stars and planets, our hearts divide The cosmic dance, a rhythm so fine

Our love's gravity, warps time and space in line

On Mars' red soil, our footsteps entwine A love so strong, like a cosmic vine Through the void, our hearts beat as one In the silence, our love has just begun

Ramesh Mofleh, a cosmic name

Our love's constellation, forever in flame.

Ramesh Mofleh Hussaini

Whispers of the Night

The stars up high, a twinkling sea A celestial map, for dreams to be

The moon's soft glow, a gentle light

Guides me through darkness, to morning's delight

In this quiet hour, I find my voice

A whispered prayer, a heartfelt choice To let go fears, and doubts that roam

And find solace, in the stillness of the home

The world outside, a busy throng But in my heart, a peaceful song A melody of hope, a rhythm true

A symphony of love, that echoes anew

In the stillness, I find my way

Through life's labyrinth, to a brighter day Where love and joy, entwined in bliss

A haven of peace, where heart and soul kiss.

Ramesh Mofleh Hussaini

8
Echoes of Longing

In the depths of my soul, a flame burns bright

A yearning for connection, a love so true and light

It's the echo of memories, of moments shared with glee A bittersweet reminder, of what's been and what could be

In the silence, I hear your voice

A whispered promise, a heartfelt choice To follow the path, where love will lead

Through life's labyrinth, to a place of peace and need

The stars above, a celestial sea

A twinkling canvas, of infinite possibility

They whisper secrets, of the universe's design

A mysterious language, that only love can divine

In the stillness, I find my way

Through life's turbulence, to a brighter day Where love's warm light, will guide me home And in your arms, my heart will find its own.

Ramesh Mofleh Hussaini

9
It Seems

It seems every side of me is surrounded by dragons' might This fatherless pain, oh God, is without a cure in sight

I'm entangled in problems and anxieties, and none can ease

My fate's ruined, full of stories, and a heart that's lost its peace

If you're happy with my heart's wounds, it's a strange delight This heart of mine is broken, and silent, without a fight

My cry has reached the throat of the same sky above

Though your heart and ears belong to God, a plea of endless love

Ramesh, what dream did you see tonight?

The presence of someone like you, in the depths of solitude's plight.

Ramesh Mofleh Hussaini

10

No one but your love resides in my heart's chest

I'll cry out, shed tears, but there's no one to help, no rest I've
become Majnun, wandered to your valley's side

No one's with me, it seems there's no one like God to abide

Every corner, I search for you, everywhere I've strayed

My heart's lost, your love's the one thing that's not mislaid One
day, you'll know the secret of my heart's pain Knowing our
love's not a bad thing, it's love's sweet refrain

The pen must write of pain and cry, of verse and prose

There's no one but poetry and pen to hold, Ramesh's woes.

Ramesh Mofleh. Hussaini

11
Moonlit Serenade

The moon casts shadows on the wall A silver glow, that echoes
all

The whispers of the night, a gentle breeze That stirs the heart,
and brings us to our knees

In this quiet hour, I find my voice A melody, that makes some
noise A serenade, that speaks of love

A heart that's beating, sent from above

The stars up high, a twinkling sea A celestial map, for you and
me

To navigate, the depths of our soul And find the love, that
makes us whole

In the stillness, I hear your name

A whispered promise, a love that's claimed

A bond that's strong, a heart that's true A love that's shining, just
for you.

Ramesh Mofleh Hussaini

12
You Don't Come to See Me

Why don't you visit, what's weighing on your heart? No effort to mend me, are you even a part?

If you knew my struggles, you'd see I'm lost in time

A friend's promise matters, on this long and winding climb

Memories of you linger, a treasured past Whispers of affection, a love that will forever last

Do you think of me, dear one? Am I on your mind?

A letter, a message, to soothe my heart's unrest, I'd find

If love and companionship guide your way

I'll wait for you, and your loving gaze, day by day If our paths align, take a moment to stay

And let the love we share light up the way.

Ramesh Mofleh Hussaini

13
Eternal Flame of Love

Love's fire burns deep within our soul

A flame that flickers, yet never grows old Like stormy seas, it crashes on the shore

Bringing excitement, and a love we've never known before

It's a melody that echoes through our heart A symphony of love, a work of art

In love's sweet grasp, time and space entwine Moments merge with eternity's divine

Tears become pearls, and smiles unfold Love's beauty shines, like a story yet untold Life's rhythm changes, to a sweeter beat

A love that's pure, and wild, and uniquely sweet

In love's embrace, we find our peaceful nest A haven where our hearts can rest

The flame of love, forever burns so bright Guiding us through, the darkest of nights.

Ramesh Mofleh Hussaini

14
Your Love, My Guiding Light

In your eyes, my heart finds a home A love so pure, it makes me
whole

I was lost, but your glance set me free Now, you're my Kaaba,
my destiny

In dreams, I see us entwined

A love so strong, it leaves all else behind I've searched for
solace, in empty space

But with you, my heart finds its perfect place

Your love, a flame that burns so bright Guides me through, the
darkest of nights In your arms, I find my peaceful nest With
you, my love, I am forever blessed

With every breath, I'll love you more Through every test, my
heart will adore You're the wings that lift me high

My love, my guiding light, my reason to try.

Ramesh Mofleh Hussaini

15
Eternal Bloom

In the garden of my heart, you bloom A flower so rare, in eternal perfume Your petals soft, your scent so sweet In your beauty, my soul finds retreat

Your love is the sunshine that I crave Warming my heart, and lighting my way In your eyes, I see a love so true

A love that's pure, and forever new

With every breath, I'll love you more Through every test, my heart will adore You're the melody that fills my soul

My love, my flower, my heart's goal.

Ramesh Mofleh Hussaini

16
Your Love, My Guiding Light

In your eyes, my heart finds a home A love so pure, it makes me whole

I was lost, but your glance set me free Now, you're my Kaaba, my destiny

In dreams, I see us entwined

A love so strong, it leaves all else behind I've searched for solace, in empty space

But with you, my heart finds its perfect place

Your love, a flame that burns so bright Guides me through, the darkest of nights In your arms, I find my peaceful nest With you, my love, I am forever blessed

With every breath, I'll love you more Through every test, my heart will adore

You're the wings that lift me high

My love, my guiding light, my reason to try.

Ramesh Mofleh Hussaini

17
Eternal Bloom

In the garden of my heart, you bloom A flower so rare, in eternal perfume Your petals soft, your scent so sweet In your beauty, my soul finds retreat

Your love is the sunshine that I crave Warming my heart, and lighting my way In your eyes, I see a love so true

A love that's pure, and forever new

With every breath, I'll love you more Through every test, my heart will adore You're the melody that fills my soul

My love, my flower, my heart's goal.

Ramesh Mofleh Hussaini

18
Whispers of Time

In fleeting moments, love shines bright A flash of beauty, in the
passage of night

Time, a thief, steals away our prime

Leaving memories, like autumn's leaves in time

Yet, in your eyes, my heart finds a home

A refuge from life's storms, where love is known Your touch
ignites a flame, that burns so true Guiding me through, life's
joys and sorrows anew

Like a river's flow, our love will find its way Through life's
twists and turns, come what may In your love, I find my
peaceful nest

With you, my heart beats best

<u>Ramesh Mofleh Hussaini</u>

19
'Echoes of Longing

In the silence, my heart beats for you A rhythm of love, that's forever true Like a river's flow, my tears fall deep

Longing for your touch, my soul to keep

In the darkness, your memory shines bright

A guiding light, that leads me through the night With every breath, I'll love you more

Through every test, my heart will adore

Like a bird set free, my soul takes flight In your love, I find my peaceful night With you by my side, I feel complete

Together we'll dance, to love's gentle beat.

Ramesh Mofleh Hussaini

20
Echoes of the Soul

In the depths of my heart, a whisper calls A gentle breeze that
stirs the walls

Of memories past, of love and pain

A symphony that echoes through my brain

Like a river's flow, my thoughts drift free A reflection of the
soul's dark sea

In the silence, I search for a light

A guiding star that shines through the night

With every breath, I'll find my way

Through life's labyrinth, I'll seize the day And though the path
may twist and turn My heart will beat, with love that yearns.

Ramesh Mofleh Hussaini

21
The Poet's Wish

If only words could paint the heart A canvas of emotions, a work of art I'd weave a tale of love and pain

A symphony of verse, that echoes through the brain

But words are fragile, like autumn leaves They wither fast, and memories deceive Yet still I write, in hope and in despair

A poet's quest, to capture life's fleeting air

In every line, a piece of me resides

A fragment of soul, that love and grief divide

I'll keep on writing, through joy and through strife For in the words, I'll find my life.

<u>Ramesh Mofleh Hussaini</u>

22
Rebel Heart

In the shadows, a fire burns

A flame of defiance, that yearns

To break free from chains that bind To shatter norms, and leave the grind

With every step, I claim my ground A rebel's spirit, that's unbound

My heart beats strong, with a voice that's clear I'll speak my truth, without a fear

In a world that's gray, I'll be the hue A splash of color, that breaks through

I'll dance with passion, and sing with glee A rebel's heart, that's wild and free.

Ramesh Mofleh Hussaini

23
A Cry for Justice

In a land of shadows, where freedom fades A cry for justice, in sorrow's shades

The people suffer, in silence and pain Their voices silenced, their rights in vain

The schools are closed, the future's unsure The enemy's cruelty, we can't endure

Years of bloodshed, and hearts turned cold Longing for peace, our souls grow old

I'll speak out loud, against the pain and strife For justice and equality, I'll fight for life

Being a girl, a daughter, is not a crime

Ramesh Mofleh Hussaini

24
"Heartbeat"

In the rhythm of your heartbeat, I find my home A place where love resides, and I am never alone The pulse of your affection, a symphony so fine A melody that echoes, deep within my mind

With every beat, our hearts entwine A dance of love, a love divine

In your eyes, my soul finds rest A love so strong, it forever lasts

Ramesh Mofleh Hussaini

This is good in the back of the book

A letter to my self

In the depths of my soul, a love lies hidden,

Like a secret tucked away in the pages of my heart. I've fallen in love with my own imagination,

A world I've created in my mind, where love is real, Even if it's not in reality.

I don't want to wake up from this sweet dream, I don't want to see the bitter truth of reality.

My heart yearns for the love you didn't have,

For the person who only existed in my imagination, For the moments that passed in my mind,

For the smiles I saw in my dreams.

I still love you with all my being,

With all my heart. I swear to the love that never was, But lives in my heart. I swear to the moments we had, In the world of

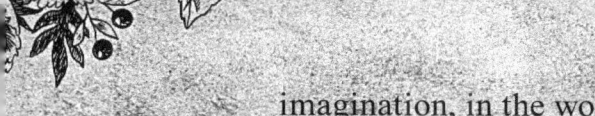

imagination, in the world of dreams.

Let me be happy with my dreams, Let me live in my own world,

Where love is real, where there's no pain or suffering, Where there's only love and affection.

I'm still in love with that imaginary person, In love with the love I never had.

In this world of imagination,

I see you, I want you, I love you.

I don't want to wake up from this dream, Because in this world, my love is real.

My dream is long, full of hope and aspirations, Full of love and affection.

Let me stay in this dream,

Let me live with my imagination. Because in this world, I'm free, Free to love, free to cherish.

And in this freedom, I'm happy, Happy in my world of imagination. Let me die in this dream.

I have my own paradise.

What do I care about your paradise?

In your paradise, my dream doesn't exist, I'm not there. Let me die in my own dreams, In my own imagination, while I'm still alive,

But not with you, not in your world. I'm not there. I'm at peace in my own dream.

Ramesh Mofleh Hussaini

26
This is about me

In a distant and unknown land, where poetry was hanged and love was stoned with heavy rocks, life flowed like a bitter and silent river. In this land, kindness was crossed out, and women lived with fear and anxiety, as if darkness could descend upon them at any moment and drag them into destruction.

In my land, women are not recognized as women; they are called "black-headed," "weak," and "animal." Children's rights and women's rights are like autumn leaves that have fallen to the ground and withered. Humans are not recognized as humans; it's as if humanity is a forgotten concept.

Women are deprived of the right to education, work, freedom, dance, write poetry, take pictures, and even laugh; it's as if their lips have been stripped of smiles and replaced with tears. From the moment I knew my left and right hands, there was war; an endless war where humans were killing each other, and their cries were stuck in their throats.

People were torn apart in the name of religion, under the banner of Islam; it's as if religion had become a pretext for war, killing, and rape. Racial, gender, and ethnic discrimination was like a fire that burned brighter every day, turning humanity into ashes.

I am Ramesh; a melody of pain and suffering from this land, stuck in my throat. I want to scream; a scream that would shake the heavens, but my voice is suffocated; like a bird whose wings are tied and can't fly.

Wherever I go, my bad luck precedes me; it's as if my fate is chained. I wanted to change my country, so I migrated; my name became "migrant." An Afghan migrant is the most wretched human in the world; someone whose language, culture, and identity are violated.

In every place I am, I am infamous as a terrorist; it's as if terrorism is engraved on my forehead. Even if you're the most worthy human on earth, it's enough to know you're

Afghan; then everything changes. People's looks change, their behavior changes, and they see you as a second-class human.

I am Ramesh, an Afghan migrant; my pain and suffering are endless; a story that never ends and drags me into nowhere. In this land, childhood and adolescence are strange and unknown words; it's as if childhood doesn't exist, and adolescence has no meaning.

Our biography is a bitter tragedy that never ends; a story that drags us into nowhere. I am a scroll of pain and suffering; a story that never ends, starting from nowhere and reaching nowhere. A journey without end in a land without a name or sign, where life means pain, suffering, and prison; living under the heavy shadow of oppression and injustice.

But I still hope; I hope for a day when women's and men's rights are equal, and humans are recognized as humans. I am a fighter; I won't give up on fighting and hope. As long as I have breath in my chest, I'll fight for freedom and equality; for a life that is worthy of humanity.

I, Ramesh, scream with all my being; a scream that maybe someone will hear, maybe someone will understand. I, Ramesh, hope with all my heart; I hope for a day when no human will be oppressed, no woman will be oppressed, and no child will be in war and killing.

Ramesh Mofleh Hussaini

I, am a fighter.

27
"Unspoken"

In the silence, whispers echo

A world unseen, where hearts are locked The wind carries secrets, untold stories

Of dreams that withered, like autumn's glory

In this quiet, shadows dance and play

A melancholy waltz, where hope fades away The stars above, a distant hum

A lullaby, for the lost and numb

Yet, in the stillness, a spark remains A flicker of light, that refuses to wane

A beacon in darkness, a heart that beats A testament to love, that secretly meets

Ramesh Mofleh Hussaini

28
"Echoes of Pain"

In my heart, a sorrow resides

A weight that presses, deep inside The world outside, a distant hum A melody, of pain to come

The skies are gray, the winds do moan A reflection, of the heart's deep tone The words I speak, a cry, a plea

A call for help, for you and me

But still I hold, on to hope

A light that shines, a way to cope

A beacon bright, in the darkest night A guiding star, that leads to new light

Ramesh Mofleh Hussaini

29
"Eco de dolor"

En mi corazo´n, un dolor reside

Un peso que oprime, profundo dentro El mundo exterior, un
rumor lejano Una melodí´a, de dolor que viene

Los cielos esta´n grises, los vientos gimen Un reflejo, del tono
profundo del corazo´n Las palabras que hablo, un grito, un ruego
Un llamado de ayuda, para ti y para mí´

En este mundo, donde el amor es una prueba

Donde los corazones se rompen, y las almas encuentran
descanso Busco consuelo, una brisa suave

Un calmante dentro, de las tormentosas olas

Pero au´n sostengo, la esperanza

Una luz que brilla, una forma de afrontar Un faro brillante, en la
noche ma´s oscura

Una estrella guí´a, que conduce a una nueva luz

Ramesh Mofleh Hussaini

30
"Hidden Smile"

Tears fall like rain Yet I smile again Pain hides behind A fragile grin.

Ramesh Mofleh Hussaini

31
"Longing"

In your absence, I wait

A heart that beats, a love that's late Time stands still, my soul astray Longing for your loving way.

Ramesh Mofleh Hussaini

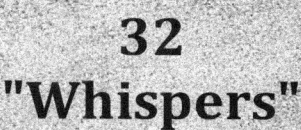

32
"Whispers"

In the silence, I hear your voice

A whispered promise, a heartfelt choice Fading echoes, memories remain Longing for love that could not stay.

Ramesh Mofleh Hussaini

33
"Fleeting Dreams"

I built a castle in the air

A love that wasn't meant to share A story spun, a heart that broke

A dream that faded, a soul that spoke.

من قلعهای در هوا ساختم عشقی که قرار نبود سهیم باشم

داستانی بافتم، قلبی شکست رویایی که محو شد، روحی که سخن گفت

Ramesh Mofleh Hussaini

34

"Perhaps in fate's design, we're not aligned, Yet my heart beats for you, a love so divine. Yesterday's whispers, today's tender sighs,

Tomorrow's dreams, where love's sweet surprise.

In fleeting moments, I see your face,

A love so pure, a heartfelt, sacred space. Though destiny may keep us far apart,

My love for you remains, a constant in my heart."

"Maybe we're not meant to be, But my love for you is all I see. Yesterday, today, and forever true,

Hoping someday, my heart belongs to you."

Ramesh Mofleh Hussaini

35

"Maybe we're not meant to be, But my love for you is all I see. Yesterday, today, and forever true,

Hoping someday, my heart belongs to you.

<u>Ramesh Mofleh Hussaini</u>

36

In the land where women's rights are fought, Afghan sisters
brave, strong, and unbowed. Their voices rise, their courage
sought,

Yet their freedoms remain in shadowed shroud.

With grace and resilience, they stand tall, Challenging barriers,
breaking down walls. In a world where traditions enthrall,

They seek justice, refusing to fall.

Oh, Afghan women with hearts so bold,

Your stories untold, your struggles untold. May your voices
echo, may your stories unfold, Empowered, respected, and
honored in gold.

Let the world hear your mighty roar, As you fight for equality,
forever more. Oh, Afghan women, beacon of light,

May your dreams take flight, shining bright.

Ramesh Mofleh Hussaini

37

A leader stands, with vision grand

Freedom's call, across this land

For Afghan girls, a brighter day

Where knowledge shines, and hope finds way

With every step, a promise made

To bring forth change, to pave the shade

Of Taliban's darkness, lost and cold

And bring the light, where hearts can unfold

In unity, we stand as one

Long live the hope, that guides us through

A brighter future, for me and you

Ramesh Mofleh Hussaini

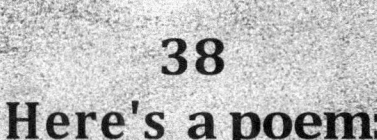

38
Here's a poem:

Afghan girls rise, with hearts so bright,

In a land of struggle, they shine with light. Their pens write
stories of hope and might,

A future brighter, where freedom takes flight.

With every step, they claim their ground, Their voices rising, a
powerful sound.

They fight for rights, for a life untamed,

Their resilience, a beacon that's proclaimed.

In the face of challenge, they stand tall, Their courage inspiring,
one and all.

Their hearts ablaze, with a fire so true,

Afghan girls, a force, that will see them through.

Their dreams are big, their spirits bold,

They'll shape their future, with hearts of gold. Their story's
being written, with every line,

A tale of strength, of a spirit divine.

Ramesh Mofleh Hussaini

39

"Your touch ignites a flame so deep, A heart divided, in love's dark sleep. I search for answers, night and day,

Only God knows what's meant to stay.

In heart's despair, I'm lost and blind, Darkness surrounds, and I'm left behind. Time loses all meaning, day and night,

My soul yearns for you, a constant fight.

Shyness hides my heart, my love unseen, Passion's a storm, wild and unclean.

In your eyes, my soul finds peace, Without you, I'm lost, my heart releases."

Ramesh Mofleh Hussaini

"Moonlit whispers, shadows play, A heart beats fast, in secret way. Love's gentle touch, a tender flame,

In darkness shines, with love's sweet name."

Ramesh Mofleh Hussaini

41"Moonlit whispers, shadows play,

A heart beats fast, in secret way.

Love's gentle touch, a tender flame,

In darkness shines, with love's sweet name."

Ramesh Mofleh Hussaini

41

"Dreams weave a gentle, loving spell,

In slumber's realm, our hearts can dwell. Though apart, you're close to me,

In dreams, our love shines wild and free.

Sweet whispers echo, a tender tone, Longing's flame burns, all its own. In moonlit nights, I'll hold you tight,

In dreams, our love takes gentle flight.

Until we meet, know you're adored,

In dreams, our hearts beat, forever more."

Ramesh Mofleh Hussaini

42

Softly falls the evening dew, A gentle hush, a peaceful hue.

The stars appear, like diamonds bright, In the night sky, a wondrous sight.

The world is calm, in quiet sleep,

Dreams unfold, secrets they keep. The moon's soft glow, a gentle beam, Illuminates, a peaceful dream.

Ramesh Mofleh Hussaini

43

"My heart betrayed, I heeded its call, Led astray, I took the fatal fall.

No remedy, but tears to confess, Regret and sorrow, my eternal stress."

Ramesh Mofleh Hussaini

44

"My heart betrayed, I heeded its call, Led astray, I took the fatal fall.

Regret and sorrow, my constant guest, No remedy, but tears to confess.

I listened to my heart's desire,

And now I'm left with love's dark fire. No escape, no solace to be found,

My heart, a prisoner, forever bound."

"I erred, my heart did stray, Deceitful whispers led the way. No turning back, I'm lost in pain,

A lesson learned, in love's sweet game."

Ramesh Mofleh Hussaini

45
A Letter to Myself

In the depths of my soul lies a love, hidden like a secret, concealed between the pages of my heart. I fell in love with my own imaginings, with the world I created in my mind—a world where love is real, even if it does not exist in reality. I do not wish to wake from this sweet dream; I do not want to face the bitter truth of reality.

My heart longs for a love i never had, for someone who existed only in my imagination, for moments that passed in my dreams, for smiles I only saw in visions. I still love you—with all my being, with all my heart. I swear by the love that never became real, yet lives within me. I swear by the moments we shared together, in the world of imagination, in the world of dreams.

Let me be happy with my dreams, let me live in my own world—a place where love is true, where there is no pain or sorrow, where only love and kindness exist. I am still in love with that imagined person, in love with a love I never attained.

In this world of dreams, I see you, I want you, I love you. I do not want to leave this dream, for here my love is real. My dream is vast, filled with hope and longing, filled with love and tenderness.

Let me remain in this dream, let me live with my visions. For in this world, I am free—free to love, free to give my heart. And in this freedom, I am happy—happy in the world of my imagination.

Let me die in this dream; I already have my own paradise.
What need have I for your paradise, when in your heaven my
dream does not exist, and I am not there? Let me die in

my soaring visions, in my own dreams—alive, yet not with you.
I am not there. I am within my dream.

Ramesh Mofleh Hussaini

"I have no choice, I'm forced to adapt,

I'll get used to being a shadow on the wall, a mere habit. You don't know the secrets of this habit, but I'll endure, Living in exile, far from my loved one, I'll make it my nature.

Everyone else kisses their beloved's lips,

But I'll get accustomed to my pillow and cigarette's bitter grip. Oh, God, what's destined for me? I'll adapt to this fate,

I'll find solace in loving you, and this behavior I'll create.

My pen will sing your praise, my poetry's king,

I'll get used to putting my thoughts on paper, my constant thing. My loved one wounds me with harsh words, unaware of my pain, I'm a stranger, a hard habit to break, I'll endure in vain."

"With no escape, I'll learn to abide,

A shadow on the wall, my heart will reside. In foreign lands, I'll find a way to survive,

Without my love, I'll adapt, and learn to thrive.

Others find solace in love's tender kiss,

I'll find comfort in my smoke, and lonely bliss. Oh, God, what's my fate? I'll follow your will, And find solace in love, and habits that chill.

My words will flow, a poetic stream,

I'll put my heart on paper, my only dream. My love may wound me, with words so cold, But I'll endure, a stranger, growing old."

Ramesh Mofleh Hussaini

47

"I'm restless, like lovers, oh my heart,

I'm a wanderer, without love, I'm torn apart. Oh my rose,
wherever I go, I'm sorrowful,

My cup doesn't hold wine or cigarette, just memories of you,
unforgettable.

Wherever I look, no one's by my side,

I'm repentant of everyone and everything, I've lost my guide.
Everyone's got companions, friends and brothers,

But I'm alone, in this exile, what do I have?

I'm waiting for you, Ramesh, but I'm afraid,

Of the silence that's endless, my heart's dismayed."

Ramesh Mofleh Hussaini

48

"In love's colors, I'm restless and blue,

Longing for connection, with a heart that's true. Like a rose in bloom, I wander, lost and alone,

My heart's cup empty, but memories of you remain, like a sweet tone.

Every face I see, is a stranger's gaze,

I'm repentant of the world, in this endless maze. Others have friends, and loved ones by their side, But I'm a wanderer, in exile, with no place to reside.

I'm waiting for you, my love, my heart's desire, But the silence is deafening, my soul on fire.

In this desolate land, I'm searching for a friend, A love that's true, that will never end."

Ramesh Mofleh Hussaini

49

When longing takes over my entire being, the toughest moments of life unfold. As the evening falls, my heart becomes heavy, and loneliness intensifies the yearning. Exile and silence are the bitter companions of this longing. There's no one to lean on, I have to embrace myself. The pain of longing is so overwhelming that it feels like they're playing with my love and heart, and I keep pretending not to understand. In this game, my heart

breaks over and over. I still hope that maybe tomorrow will be a different day, a day of your presence beside me. Memories of the past are etched on my soul like wilted petals. Every time I recall the good times with you, the pain and longing become fresher. I hide my

longing with tears, but my tears silently scream. When night falls, silence fills the house, and I search for a refuge for my heart in the darkness. Behind every smile, there are thousands of pains and sorrows hidden. The pain of loneliness, the pain of longing, the pain of not having someone to listen, understand, and empathize. I am so alone, so longing. I

thought I had love, but I didn't. I thought you were my brother, but you weren't. I thought you were my sister, but you were my enemy. I am very lonely, the one who betrayed me was the one who slept beside me. Who should I tell? I told you. God hears my voice, but He didn't. My heart is heavy, my heart is heavy. I don't scream, I remain silent. I didn't cry. I tell you, oh star that perhaps my longing is you every night. I tell you, oh waters of the sea that perhaps the drops of blood from my broken heart are you. Are you with me, or are you gone too? I, Ramish, am drowning in this loneliness with longing. There's no one to listen, no one to understand. There's only silence, tears, and pain. In this cruel world, I only hear the footsteps of loneliness rushing towards the future. Longing has engulfed my entire being

like a thick fog. I don't know how to get out of this boundless sea, how to escape this endless pain. When night falls, the stars in the sky shine like my tears. The sea waves and takes my cries to the depths. There's no one to hear, no one to understand. There's only silence, pain, and tears. Sometimes I think maybe if I write, if I pour my pains onto paper,

some of the weight on my heart might lift. But words are powerless, they can't express the depth of my pain. Who am I longing for? Which love? Which memories? Which story? I created it, I wove it, I lost it, I became longing. I'm longing for my dreams, longing for a love that never was. In this loneliness, I only have myself and memories that grow older day by day, but their pain never fades. I, Ramish, am drowning in this boundless sea of pain and

longing. Is there anyone to save me?

<u>Ramesh Mofleh Hussaini</u>

50

"Loneliness is my sanctuary, a place where silence whispers the murmurs of my heart. In this profound stillness, I spend moments as if no one else knows my secrets. How beautiful it is to sip hot tea in this solitude and savor the moments with a cigarette, as if time has paused in this very moment. The sea is the keeper of my secrets, holding my heart's words in trust, and the sky looks at my solitude with a gaze of longing, for it too yearns for such moments. God is steadfast in His solitude because He has no love to betray, no one to break

His heart; He always finds peace in the pinnacle of His loneliness. I celebrate my solitude, at least once a year, in my seclusion, I hold a festival and inform no one, for in this celebration, it's just me and myself. If one day I die, write on my obituary card, 'I came alone, I leave

alone,' so there will be no mistake. I am a stranger, a wanderer, and in this long journey, I walk alone."

Ramesh Mofleh Hussaini

"In the silence of my heart, a melody is played—a symphony of longing for a love that is far away. In the whispers of the night, I seek solace, but the shadows only echo the emptiness of my fate. The stars above, a canvas of twinkling lights, remind me of dreams that still soar. Yet, like a fleeting breeze, my hopes fade, leaving me with the pain of unfinished love. In this empty space, I find myself lost and alone—a traveler without a map, searching for a place to call home. The love I yearn for is a mirage on the horizon—a promise of happiness that is always distant, yet I cling to it. Perhaps in the quiet hours, when darkness reigns, I'll find the courage to let go of these enduring pains. And though the love I seek may never be

mine, its essence will forever shine within the depths of my soul."

Ramesh Mofleh Hussaini

52

"The love I don't have is a dream I nurture in my mind, a feeling alive in my heart but nonexistent in reality. I long for someone who's not here, yearning to touch hands I've never held. This love I don't have is like an unfinished painting, lingering in my mind, never

complete. If only there was someone beside me to experience love with, but they're not here."

<u>Ramesh Mofleh Hussaini</u>

53

"In the depths of my soul, your light shines bright, A moonlit glow that guides me through the night. I pray you're spared my troubles and my pain,

Forever lost in the beauty of your gaze, where love remains.

Time has passed, and I'm now craving your sight, Your eyes, a brief encounter on life's journey tonight.

Memories of our nights linger, my heart adrift in space, Yearning for your touch, the warmth of your loving face.

In dreams, I see our story unfold,

A tale of love, of trials, of life's duality to hold."

<u>Ramesh Mofleh Hussaini</u>

"Love is like an endless poem,

A moment where time stands still, and the world is just two souls. Love is a feeling that makes the heart dance and the spirit soar.

It's like a romantic poem, each verse promising a lifetime of emotion and affection.

You, my love, are like a sweet ghazal,

With smiles, tears, hopes, and dreams woven into your words. Your gaze brings the poem of love to life in my heart,

And the touch of your hand choreographs a dance of joy in my soul.

In your arms, I find security and peace,

As if I'm in a small paradise with my true partner. With every kiss, our love ignites,

And with every glance, we journey deeper into each other's hearts.

Your love has taken me to a new world,

A world where nothing matters except you and our love. You captivate my heart with a smile,

And set my soul beating with a single look.

My love for you is endless and infinite, Like a river that never dries up.

With you, I forget the moments and immerse myself in love.

You're the one who has defined love in its truest sense for me."

Ramesh Mofleh Hussaini

55

"In the silence of endless nights, I count my longings, And with each count, I whisper your name.

My heart yearns for you, dear companion,

Like leaves that fall from the tree in autumn, I'm lost and alone.

In this exile, I hear only the sound of your footsteps, Echoing through the alleys of memories, coming and going.

I miss your smile, your words, everything that made sense with you by my side. I love you, dear companion, I'm longing for you,

Come and save me from this loneliness."

Ramesh Mofleh Hussaini

56

"In whispers, I hoped my verse would be his, A balm for his soul, a gentle kiss.

I yearned to break free from this cage of pain, And let my heart beat solely for him, in vain.

With tender words, I greet you, my love so true, Hoping they'd reach the hearts of nobles, too.

In darkest nights, I wished my voice would flow, And in his soul, my words would gently glow.

My poem tells your story, yet I wished it would bring, A smile to your lips, a joy that clings.

Your memory stays with me, a bittersweet refrain,

Oh, how I longed for my love to be plain."

Ramesh Mofleh Hussaini

57

"With pen and notebook, my heart finds a friend, A confidant in verse, where emotions blend.

I seek a remedy for my soul's deep wound,

A poet's burning words, my heart's profound.

Ramish's lament echoes, a cry to the air, A couplet that unveils the secrets I share. Separation's weight I cannot bear,

My pen sketches the portrait of my despair.

With hidden scars, Ramish Mofleh sings his tale, Of love and longing, a heart that fails.

Read the couplet, let it reach the heart of my dear,

Perhaps, in verse, our souls will meet, and love will appear."

Ramesh Mofleh Hussaini

58

"You didn't give me your heart, but with you near, At least be
kind to my sorrow, calm my fear.

Every message you send isn't love, I know,

But when you're by my side, at least let your love show.

I'm enchanted by your nature, gentle and kind, Like Layli's
love, a beauty to behold, one of a kind. Oh Lord, forgive
Ramish, for he's lost his way,

I'm a madman, but at least you're my idol, every day.

My dreams are filled with you, my heart's delight,

At least sit with me, and make this night feel just right."

Ramesh Mofleh Hussaini

"In a distant and unknown land, where poetry was silenced and love was stoned with heavy rocks, life flowed like a bitter and silent river. In this land, kindness was crossed out, and women lived in fear and anxiety, as if darkness could descend upon them at any moment and drag them into destruction. In my land, women are not recognized as women; they are called 'black-headed,' 'weak,' and 'animal.' Children's rights and women's rights are like autumn leaves that have fallen to the ground and withered. Humans are not recognized as humans; it seems humanity is a forgotten concept. Women are deprived of the right to education, work, freedom, dance, write poetry, take pictures, and even laugh; it's as if smiles have been taken from their lips and replaced with tears.

From the moment I knew my left and right hands, there was war; an endless war where humans were at each other's throats, and their cries were trapped in their throats. People were torn apart in the name of religion, under the flag of Islam; it seemed religion had become a pretext for war, killing, and rape. Racial, gender, and ethnic discrimination was

like a fire that flared up every day, turning humanity into ashes. I am Ramish; a melody of pain and suffering from this land, trapped in my throat. I want to scream; a scream that

shakes the heavens, but my voice is suffocated; like a bird whose wings are bound and cannot fly.

Wherever I go, my bad luck precedes me; as if my fate is chained. I wanted to change my country, so I migrated; my name became a migrant. An Afghan migrant is the most unfortunate human in the world; someone whose language, culture, and identity are violated. Wherever they are, they are infamous for being terrorists; as if terrorism is engraved on their forehead. Even if you're the most worthy person on earth, it's enough to know you're Afghan; then everything changes. Looks change, behavior changes, and you're seen as a second-class human.

I am Ramish, an Afghan migrant; my pain and suffering are endless; a story that never ends and drags me into nowhere. In this land, childhood and adolescence are strange and unknown words; it's as if childhood doesn't exist, and adolescence has no meaning. Our biographies are a bitter tragedy without end; a story that never ends and drags us into nowhere. I am a scroll of pain and suffering; a story without end that starts from nowhere and reaches nowhere. An endless journey in a land without a name and sign, where life

means pain, suffering, and prison; it means living under the heavy shadow of oppression and injustice.

But I still hope; hope for a day when women's and men's rights are equal, and humans are recognized as humans. I am a fighter; I won't give up on my struggle and hope. As long as I have breath in my chest, I'll fight for freedom and equality; for a life that is worthy of humanity. I, Ramish, scream with all my being; a scream that maybe someone will hear, maybe someone will understand. I, Ramish, hope with all my heart; hope for a day when no human is oppressed, no woman is oppressed, no child is in war and killing.

Ramesh Mofleh Hussaini

I am a fighter

"Afghan migrants, survivors of suffering and hope on the winding paths of fate, sometimes people are forced to leave their nests, but their homeland remains in their hearts. Afghan

migrants, who have crossed the borders of Iran, are a symbol of resilience and love for their motherland. The people of Herat, with pure hearts and helping hands, have spread a carpet of love and respect so that the feet of these tired travelers do not slip. Warm and sincere food has given them a taste of home and lit a spark of hope in their eyes.

Afghan migrants, the true inhabitants of this ancient land, with a proud history and rich culture, are not just refugees, but the true guardians of their homeland. The concept of

homeland, which resides in every human heart, is a symbol of love, pride, and resilience for them. With every step, with every breath, they keep the love for their homeland alive, even if they are in a foreign land.

Although I have lived in a foreign land for 21 years, my homeland is still my homeland. I myself have lived in America for 21 years, but the scent of Herat is still on my lips. 21 years, 21 minutes, I have not forgotten my people and my land. The love for my homeland runs through my veins, and nothing can erase this love.

The people of Herat, with their warm welcome and helping hands, have shown that humanity is still alive, and love for fellow humans is our greatest asset. This welcome is a shining light on the migrants' path, a path that is fraught with difficulties and bitterness, but with hope and resilience, one can overcome it.

In this new land, Afghan migrants have found an opportunity to start anew. An opportunity to rebuild their lives and write a new chapter of hope and dreams. We hope that in this land, you will start a new life with peace and comfort, build a bright future for yourself and your family, and always keep your homeland alive in your heart."

Ramesh Mofleh Hussaini

61

"In the depths of the night's silence, the whispers of loving hearts can be heard. The words that arise from the depths of our hearts sometimes become a balm for the hidden wounds of loving and weary hearts. Tonight, in this night of listening to the whispers of our inner selves, is an opportunity to journey into the depths of love and to heal our pains with the words that come from our hearts. In these moments, the silence of the night becomes a refuge for the unspoken cries of our love.

The words we speak sometimes become the whispers of peace that we seek. So let us listen to the whispers of our loving hearts together in this night, and with the words that arise from the depths of our being, let us find and heal love. In this night of listening to our inner whispers, we

are together to be a balm for each other's pains with the words that come from the heart. Join us and let us listen to the whispers of our loving hearts in this night and experience love together."

Ramesh Mofleh Hussaini

62

"In these lonely nights, my heart is filled with memories of a love that doesn't exist, yet it's

eternal in my mind. I think of smiles that I never saw, of hands that I never touched. I pour my longings into poetry, hoping to alleviate this endless pain. But love seems to be a toy that I don't have, and in this game, I'm just a spectator.

I walk through the quiet streets of my mind, searching for a trace of a love that never came. At every step, a voice calls out, saying "come," but alas, it's not your voice. Love has become a

legend in the book of my life, one that never reached its end, but is already finished. In this notebook of love, only one blank page remains, empty of everything I wanted to write."

Ramesh Mofleh Hussaini

63

"In the depths of lonely nights, I yearn to be in your embrace, O embodiment of love and beauty! If fate had it that we be together, you would understand that your scent is the fragrance of soul-stirring love; a scent that, like a restless spirit, reminds me of you with every breath and sets my heart aflutter.

My hands, like two birds with outstretched wings in flight, yearn to touch the warmth of your presence; so that perhaps in the soul-warming heat of your embrace, I may find peace and forget the pain of separation. In this forced exile, the only thing that keeps me alive is

the hope of seeing you; beholding your eyes, which like a turbulent sea, take me to the depths of the ocean of love and immerse me in themselves.

Oh, if only I could get lost in your eyes and find peace in your embrace, forgetting the world."

Ramesh Mofleh Hussaini

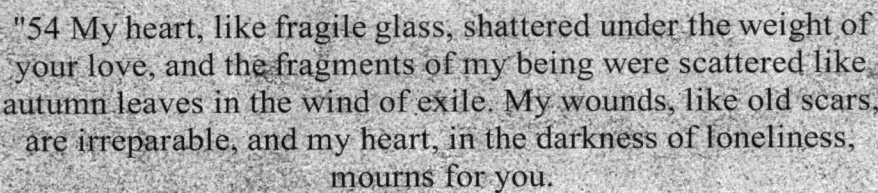

64

"54 My heart, like fragile glass, shattered under the weight of your love, and the fragments of my being were scattered like autumn leaves in the wind of exile. My wounds, like old scars, are irreparable, and my heart, in the darkness of loneliness, mourns for you.

You broke me, without knowing that breaking my heart was the end of all my hopes. Now, I am unable to gather myself, because the pieces of my existence are lost among sweet and bitter memories. Your love was like an earthquake that shook the foundation of my being, and I remain alone and bewildered in this ruin.

Farewell, O silence of my soul."

Ramesh Mofleh Hussaini

65

If I could shape the world anew,

I'd bring equality, and peace would shine through. Wars would cease, and love would be the guide, No more suffering, no more tears to hide.

I'd update ancient texts with modern might, And make humanity's heart shine bright.

One God, one faith, one love would reign, No more division, no more pain.

I'd heal the wounds of war and strife, And bring solace to a troubled life.

The sun and stars would be our friends, And travel to the cosmos would never end.

I'd make the world a garden fair,

Where love and kindness bloom and share. No more fear, no more hate, no more might, Just peace, just love, just shining light.

This is my vision, my heart's desire,

A world where love and peace conspire. May one day, humanity's dreams unfold, And the world becomes a haven to behold.

Ramesh Mofleh Hussaini

The love I don't have, a distant dream, A lie I tell myself, or so it would seem. Hard to be in love with what's not real, To pretend emotions, to fake the feel.

I'm lost in a world of make-believe, Where love's a fantasy, a distant leave.

I yearn for connection, for a gentle touch,

But it's all a ruse, a fabricated clutch.

In this false love, I'm trapped and confined, A prisoner of emotions, left behind.

The love I don't have, a haunting refrain, Echoes through my mind, a bittersweet strain.

Yet, I'll hold on to this illusion dear,

This false love that brings me fleeting cheer. For in its emptiness, I find a strange reprieve,

A moment's peace, a heart that's numb, yet alive.

Ramesh Mofleh Hussaini

"Love unseen, heart unseen, A longing deep within,

A dream of what could be, A heart that beats in vain."

Ramesh Mofleh Hussaini

68

"Love I don't have, A heart that craves, Longing for you,

In dreams, I'll stay,"

Ramesh Mofleh Hussaini

69

"Cosmic dreams, starry night,

Orbiting love, a celestial light. Gravity's pull, a heart's desire,
Lost in space, yet love's on fire."

Ramesh Mofleh Hussaini

70

When internet returns to our land,

You befriend and sync with the people's hand. All work was
stagnant, frozen in time,

Now, praise be to God, the start's sublime."

Ramesh Mofleh Hussaini

"My heart's fault, still I adore, Whatever you've done, my love's more. Loyalty or betrayal, it doesn't matter,

This heart knows only how to love you, my dear.

In your eyes, my soul finds a home, With every breath, my love will roam. Faithful or not, my heart beats for you,

Forever and always, my love shines true."

"My heart's at fault, yet love remains, Through every deed, my heart sustains.

Loyalty's weight, I choose to ignore,

For my heart's sole lesson is to love you more."

Ramesh Mofleh Hussaini

"My heart craves, with desires astray, Uncertain who to love each day.

But then I see you, and I know, Forever yours, my heart will glow.

Without you, I'd be lost and alone, But with you, my heart finds its home. I love you, my truth, my guiding light,

My love, you're not a lie, you're my delight,"

"My heart wanders, unsure and free, But with you, my love, it's meant to be. I'm lost without you, in dark and space,

With you, my heart finds its perfect place."

Ramesh Mofleh Hussaini

73

"My heart yearns for you, oh so true, If only you loved me too.

If only you were real, I'd be complete, But now I'm lost, a madman's beat.

In dreams, I see your lovely face, A fleeting thought, a wistful pace.

My madness grows, my heart does ache, Longing for you, for your love's sweet sake."

Ramesh Mofleh Hussaini

"My heart longs for you, if only you'd care, If only you were real, I'd be aware.

I'm mad with love, a heart that beats fast, Yearning for you, forever to last."

Ramesh Mofleh Hussaini

75

"My heart yearns for you, oh so true, If only you loved me too.

If only you were real, I'd be complete, But now I'm lost, a madman's beat.

In dreams, I see your lovely face, A fleeting thought, a wistful pace.

My madness grows, my heart does ache, Longing for you, for your love's sweet sake."

My heart longs for you, if only you'd care,

If only you were real, I'd be aware.

I'm mad with love, a heart that beats fast, Yearning for you, forever to last."

Ramesh Mofleh Hussaini

76

"How dim the stars without your light,

You don't speak to me, and they take flight. The stars are sulking, lost in space,

Dust of stars and sorrow fill my place.

In your absence, darkness reigns,

The stars' soft twinkle brings only pains. Their beauty's lost, their sparkle too, Without you, my heart is dark and blue."

"Stars are dim without your shine, They sulk with me, in silence divine. Dust of stars and sorrow fill my heart, Longing for you, we're worlds apart."

Ramesh Mofleh Hussaini

"Invite me to the garden of your loving arms, Where I'll kiss you till morning's gentle charms. My fingers will wander, tracing every part,

Letting world and time fade from your lovely heart."

Ramesh Mofleh Hussaini

"When starry skies I gaze upon, your eyes shine bright, When oceans vast I behold, your dreams take flight.

In slumber's realm, you're by my side,

Why then, oh why, can't you be mine, in life's tide?"

"Without you, my heart is lost and blue, Wish I had wings, to fly to you."

"My soul feels empty, my heart feels pain, Longing to be with you, to ease this strain."

Ramesh Mofleh Hussaini

79

"I love you more than words can say, In my heart, our love will always stay."

"My love for you is endless, like the sea, Forever and always, I'll be loving you, you see."

"I love you more than anything in this world, My love for you is endless, forever unfurled."

"My heart beats for you alone In your absence, I am undone Tears fall like the desert rain Longing for love that remains"

"I'll pack my tent and head to the desert's might

Beat my head against the stone, in sorrow's dark night I'll cry out loud, in longing for your face

My heart, overwhelmed, will find solace in the sea's dark place"

"In the city of night, I lose my way

Fleeing to you, my guiding star each day

My heart is heavy, weighed down with pain

You're my solace, my refuge, my heart's safe haven again"

teacher so dear, with love and care, Guiding us gently, with patience to share.

Happy Teacher's Day, a tribute to you, Thank you for all, forever true!

Why does my heart beat for one so cold? Can't it see the love that's not told?

Build me a heart of stone or steel,

One that doesn't feel, one that doesn't reveal."

"Love's flame burns bright and true,

Don't play with hearts, it's not a game to pursue. Worship with all your soul, or let be,

For love's a sacred bond, for you and

"You build arms to end humanity's strife

Yet love's fierce flame burns deeper than any knife A virus wild, no cure can tame

Love's fire rages, an endless flame"

94

"Your eyes, a canvas of dreams Your touch, a flame that beams In your arms, I find my home

Forever with you, I am never alone"

"A woman, a force so divine,

Equal in power, in heart and mind.

We build the world with hands that care, And nurture love, with every tender air.

No mere object, no silent guest,

But a voice that echoes, and a spirit that finds rest.

Like thunder in the mountains, our words will resound, And like a gentle breeze, our love will forever be found."

In exile, I'm a stranger in a foreign land My life is eternal imprisonment

My city's streets, don't see autumn Leaves fall, but I can't see their dance

Bamiyan and Badakhshan's rubies, the purple flower of Arghavan Parwan The rivers of Panjshir, all are far from me

The separation from Balkh, Nuristan, Herat The Shahnameh and art, all are in silence

My eyes witness the murder of time

Far from loved ones, sorrowful and longing A lost traveler in a foreign land

I've lost my homeland, in this point on earth

I exist, but I'm not

Ramesh Mofleh Hussaini

گل را چه که نصیب من خاری نیست در ریشهی عمر تیر و باری نیست

اینقدر چرا بخت مرا تیره نوشت ای وای خدا سرم و یک یاری نیست

گل های قشنگم همه پژمرده شدند یک شاخه گل و از کسی آثاری نیست

امروز دلم از همه عالم تنگ است قلم شد بیمار و مرا کاری نیست

یارب به کی گویم از عشق اریب دلتنگم و هیچ در کاری نیست

مردم به کجا میبرد این مقوح را رامش به کجا میبری طلداری نیست

رامش مفلح

شاعر : گویش عامیانهی شهر

What can I do with this longing?

No rose blooms in my desolate spring

My life's roots bear no fruit, no sweet delight Why is my fate so shrouded in endless night?

Oh, God, I'm lost and alone, without a guiding light My heart is weary, my soul takes flight

The flowers of joy have withered, left to decay

And I'm left with nothing, but sorrow's endless sway

My heart is heavy, my spirit worn

I search for solace, but it's hard to be heard

In this desolate landscape, I'm searching for a friend

But echoes whisper secrets, and the wind remains unbent

Oh, Love, where have you gone? I'm searching for your face

But like sand between fingers, you've slipped away, leaving empty space

Ramesh Mofleh Hussaini

www.ingramcontent.com/pod-product-compliance
Lightning Source LLC
Chambersburg PA
CBHW070828250626
47170CB00006B/2250